BUBBA THE BUSY BEAVER

BUBBA THE BUSY BEAVER

by

Judi Folmsbee

Illustrated by **Marilyn Benton**

Bubba, the Busy Beaver
Copyright © 2013 Judi Folmsbee
Second Edition 2013 (printed case)
First Edition 2003 (coil bound)
ISBN 978-1-886068-68-1
Library of Congress Control Number: 2012951546
Illustrated by Marilyn Benton
Edited by Pam Halter

Published by Fruitbearer Publishing, LLC
P.O. Box 777, Georgetown, DE 19947
302.856.6649 • FAX 302.856.7742
www.fruitbearer.com • info@fruitbearer.com
Illustrated by Marilyn Benton
Edited by Pam Halter

Printed in the United States of America

One day in early spring, Momma Beaver said to Bubba, "It's time for you to build your own lodge now, dear."

5

"Bubba, don't worry," Momma said.
"You can do it, just stick to it."

7

Bubba walked away very sad because he liked his home and didn't want to live on his own.

"What's wrong, Bubba?"
Timmy Turtle asked.

Bubba sniffled. "I have to build my own home and it's going to take a lot of work. Can you help me?"

"Sure, I can help you,"
Timmy said. "What do I do?"

Maybe you can help me carry sticks," Bubba said.
Like this." And he showed Timmy how.
S-l-o-w-l-y, Timmy picked up one little twig.

"Thank you, Timmy," Bubba said. "But
that little twig won't work for a beaver
lodge. I need to work faster than your
fine turtle legs can go. Thanks anyway."

Bubba knew
he needed more help.

He moved on and found Ollie Otter
playing on the riverbank with his
favorite sliding stone.

Bubba called to him. "Ollie, can you help me move some sticks to build a lodge?"

"Sure, just show me what to do," Ollie yelled as he slid down the riverbank with his stone. "I can do it right after I'm done sliding."

Bubba offered Ollie a hard hat. "You'll need this to be safe," he said. But Ollie was too busy playing to accept it.

Bubba chewed a branch from the tree and tossed it in the water. He watched Ollie for a minute and then turned away.

Bubba decided to move on
and found Marty Mallard.

"What's happening, Bubba?"
Marty quacked.

Bubba showed Marty some twigs. "I need to build a lodge from sticks and branches like this," he said and showed him how to stack them up tight.

"Can you help me?"
Bubba asked as he offered
Marty a hard hat.

"Sure, just let me get a little more to eat,"
Marty said. He pushed his bill into the water,
and his tail went up in the air. Marty was too
busy eating to accept the hard hat.

Bubba was now desperate to find someone else to help him. He moved on. He was tired. He rested on his tail again while he snacked on bark and leaves.

"Hi ya', Bubba," Mollie Mink squealed as she playfully jumped around in the grass.

Bubba was glad to see her. "I need help, fast! I need to build a lodge. Can you help me? It's easy. You do it like this," he said, handing Mollie a hard hat and he chewed a low branch off a tree.

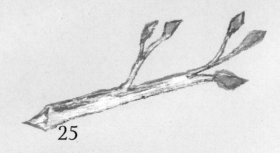

Mollie ignored the hat, so Bubba put it back on and moved into the water to demonstrate what he wanted her to do.

Mollie picked up a branch. She swayed and then fell, rolling herself into a ball around and around the branch.

"This is fun," she giggled as she rolled down a hill with the branch.

Bubba watched Mollie roll and play with the branch. He sighed. It was time to move on again.

"Murray, want to help me build a lodge?"
Bubba said. "It's easy." He showed him how.

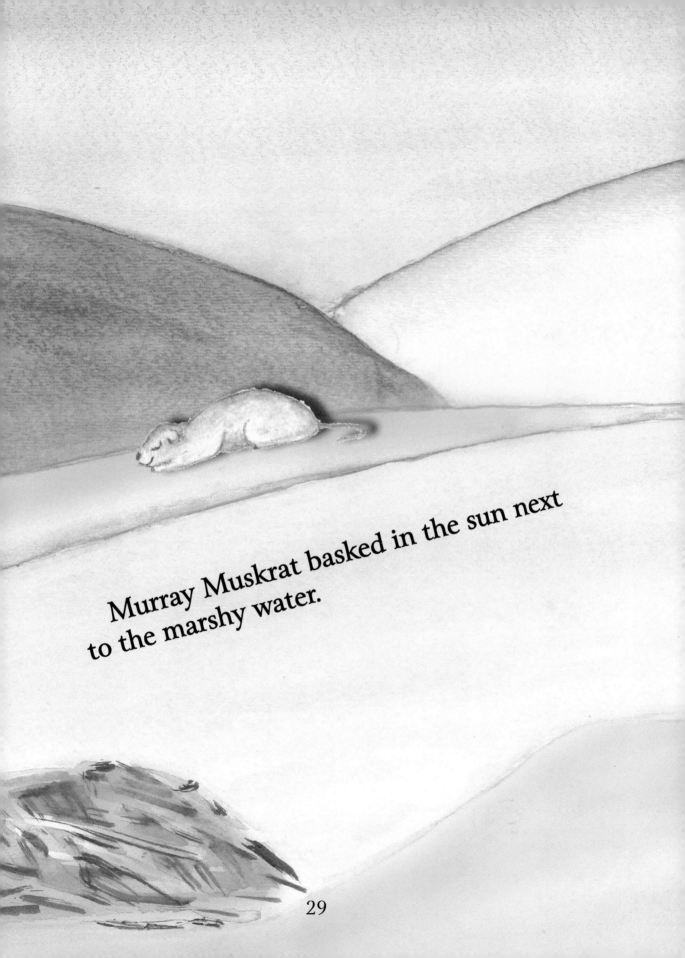

Murray Muskrat basked in the sun next to the marshy water.

29

Murray yawned. "Well, I'm drying my silvery brown coat in the sun right now. I'll help you later."

Bubba was about to give up looking.

He heard a loud squawk. It was Harriet Heron!

"Harriet, can you help me build my lodge? Like this." Bubba demonstrated.

Harriet glanced up with a big fish
n her mouth. She was clearly too
usy to help.

Again, Bubba sat on his tail for a rest. "I'll never get my lodge built," he said. He felt sad because he wanted to make his momma proud.

He heard footsteps, looked up, and saw Momma, Timmy, Ollie, Marty, Mollie, Murray and Harriet. They were all smiling at him and fully clothed!

"Bubba, you busy beaver," they shouted. "Look at the nice lodge you built!"

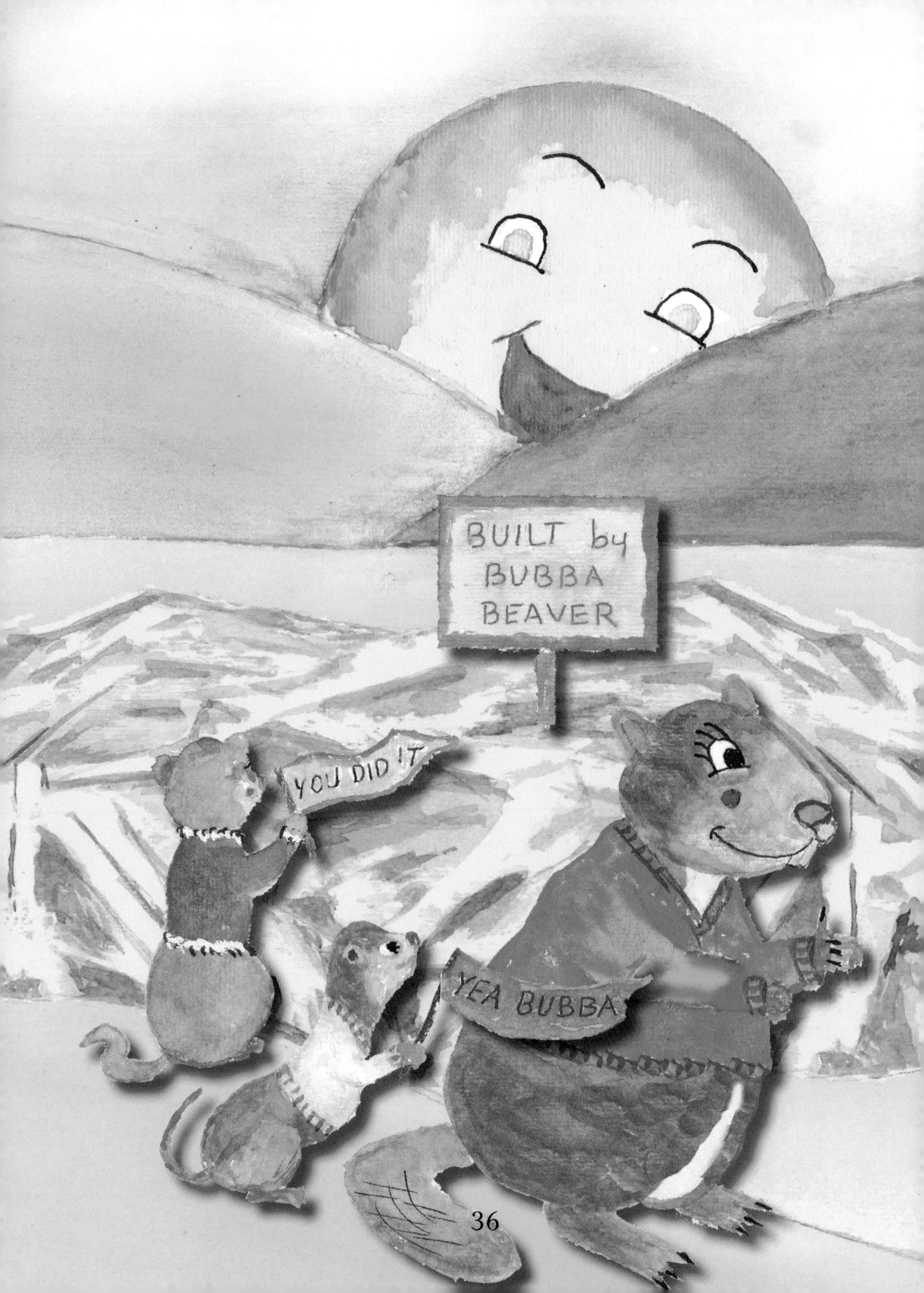
BUILT by
BUBBA
BEAVER
YOU DID IT
YEA BUBBA

Bubba worked so fast, he had not only completed the beaver lodge but had new clothes on, too! He had tried so hard to show everyone how to build a lodge that he did it himself, without any help.

"I did that?"
Bubba said.

"That's right," Momma said.
"Remember what I told you?"
Bubba laughed. "You can do it, just stick to it!"

Meet the Author

Judi Folmsbee is a retired teacher after twenty-five years in special education classrooms. She has written three children's books. Her work is published in anthologies, booklets, and newspapers. She enjoys photography, gardening, scrapbooking, family time, and her newest hobby, playing the banjo. Visit Judi at www.JudiFolmsbee.com.

Meet the Illustrator

Marilyn Benton of Cambridge, Maryland, studied art and worked as a graphic designer in Seattle and New York City. She worked as an automotive service advisor, cabinetmaker, boat carpenter, and as a missionary at a children's home in Guatemala. She began drawing and painting more seriously a few years ago. This is the first children's book that she has illustrated.

To Order

Visit www.JudiFolmsbee.com
or send your name, address, phone number, and e-mail (if applicable),
with $20.00 per hardback + $7.60 S/H to:
Judi Folmsbee
21138 Orchard Road, Ellendale, DE 19941
Please make checks payable to Judi Folmsbee.

Questions?
Call 302.684.3603 or e-mail info@judifolmsbee.com.
If you are interested in having your book(s) autographed,
please include the name(s) you want inscribed.

Discounts available through the publisher for bulk orders and fund-raisers.

Fruitbearer Publishing, LLC
P.O. Box 777, Georgetown, DE 19947
302.856.6649 • Fax 302.856.7742
info@fruitbearer.com • www.fruitbearer.com